STAR WARS

Editor - Zachary Rau
Contributing Editor - Robert Langhorn
Graphic Designers and Letterers - Tomás Montalvo-Lagos,
John Lo and Louis Csontos
Cover Designer - Gary Shum

Digital Imaging Manager - Chris Buford
Production Managers - Jennifer Miller and Mutsumi Miyazaki
Senior Designer - Anna Kernbaum
Senior Editor - Elizabeth Hurchalla
Managing Editor - Lindsey Johnston
VP of Production - Ron Klamert
Publisher & Editor in Chief - Mike Kiley
President & C.O.O. - John Parker
C.E.O. - Stuart Levy

E-mail: info@TOKYOPOP.com
Come visit us online at www.TOKYOPOP.com
Visit the official Star Wars website at www.starwars.com

A **TOKYOPOP** Cine-Manga® Book
TOKYOPOP Inc.
5900 Wilshire Blvd., Suite 2000
Los Angeles, CA 90036

Star Wars: The Phantom Menace

ISBN: 1-59532-975-7

First TOKYOPOP® printing: November 2005

10 9 8 7 6 5 4 3 2 1

Printed in Italy

STAR WARS

EPISODE I
THE PHANTOM MENACE

STORY AND SCREENPLAY BY
GEORGE LUCAS

HAMBURG • LONDON • LOS ANGELES • TOKYO

DARTH MAUL:
APPRENTICE TO SIDIOUS

DARTH SIDIOUS:
LORD OF THE SITH

OBI-WAN KENOBI:
JEDI, APPRENTICE
TO QUI-GON JINN

QUI-GON JINN:
JEDI MASTER

YODA:
SENIOR MEMBER OF
THE JEDI COUNCIL

QUEEN AMIDALA:
LEADER OF THE NABOO

JAR JAR BINKS:
A MEMBER OF
THE AMPHIBIOUS
SPECIES ON NABOO

NUTE GUNRAY:
VICEROY OF
THE TRADE
FEDERATION

SENATOR PALPATINE:
NABOO'S REPRESENTATIVE
AT THE GALACTIC SENATE

ANAKIN SKYWALKER:
SLAVE BOY

C-3PO:
PROTOCOL
DROID BUILT
BY ANAKIN

R2-D2:
ASTROMECH
DROID

A long time ago in a galaxy far far away....

Turmoil has engulfed the Galactic Republic. The taxation of trade routes to outlying star systems is in dispute.

Hoping to resolve the matter with a blockade of deadly battleships, the greedy Trade Federation has stopped all shipping to the small planet of Naboo.

While the Congress of the Republic endlessly debates this alarming chain of events, the Supreme Chancellor has secretly dispatched two Jedi Knights, the guardians of peace and justice in the galaxy, to settle the conflict....

With all due respect, the Ambassadors for the Supreme Chancellor wish to board immediately.

Yes, of course. As you know, our blockade is perfectly legal and we'd be happy to receive the Ambassadors.

THE SHIP DOCKS AND THE JEDI ARE ESCORTED TO A MEETING ROOM.

Master, how do you think this Trade Viceroy will deal with the Chancellor's demands?

These Federation types are cowards. The negotiations will be short.

This scheme of yours has failed, Lord Sidious. The blockade is finished! We dare not go against the Jedi!

This turn of events is unfortunate. We must accelerate our plans. Begin landing your troops.

My Lord, is that...legal?

I will make it legal.

And the Jedi...?

The Chancellor should not have brought them into this. Kill them, immediately!

Yes! Yes, My Lord! As you wish!

WITH GREAT STEALTH, OBI-WAN AND QUI-GON MAKE THEIR WAY BACK TO THE HANGAR, ONLY TO FACE A FEARSOME SIGHT...
It's an invasion army!
We've got to warn the Naboo and contact Chancellor Valorum. Let's split up, stow aboard separate ships and meet down on the planet.
MEANWHILE, ON THE PLANET'S SURFACE, QUEEN AMIDALA IS HOLDING COUNCIL IN THE PALACE THRONE ROOM.
We've lost all communication with the Senate on Coruscant.
A communication disruption can only mean one thing. Invasion!

Ex-squeeze-me, but de mostest safest place would be Gunga City. Is where I grew up. 'Tis a hidden city.

Can you take us there?

Uhhh, on second thought, no. My afraid my've been banished. The Bosses would do terrible tings to me. Terrrrible tings to me, if me goin' back there.

You hear that? That is the sound of a thousand terrible things heading this way.

And if they find us, they will crush us into tiny pieces and blast us into oblivion!

You-sa point is well seen. This way!

JAR JAR LEADS THE JEDI TO A LARGE SWAMP.

Wee-sa goin' underwater, okeyday? My warning you, Gungans no likin' outsiders, so don't 'spect a warm welcome.

Oh, don't worry. This hasn't been our day for warm welcomes.

AFTER APPLYING THEIR BREATHING APPARATUS AND DIVING IN, THE JEDI ARE GREETED BY THE BREATHTAKING SIGHT OF A VAST, LUMINOUS UNDERWATER CITY.

SWIMMING AHEAD, JAR JAR GUIDES THEM TO A LARGE PORTAL IN ONE OF THE DOMES.

A droid army is about to attack the Naboo. We must warn them.

You-sa cannot bees here. This army of mechineeks up dare is not our problem!

Once those droids take control of the surface, they will take control of you. You must understand this!

Mee-sa no tink so. They not know of us.

Then speed us on our way.

Wee-sa ganna speed yous away. Wee-sa give you-sa una bongo.

THE GROUP BOARDS A GUNGAN SUB AND CONTINUES ON THEIR JOURNEY TO THEED CITY, HOME OF THE NABOO.

ABOVE NABOO, THE NEIMOIDIANS ARE UPDATING DARTH SIDIOUS ON THEIR PROGRESS.

The invasion is on schedule, My Lord, but the Queen has great faith that the Senate will side with her.

Queen Amidala is young and naïve. You will find that controlling her will not be difficult.

THE HOLOGRAM FLICKERS FOR A MOMENT AND IS GONE.

You didn't tell him about the missing Jedi!

No need to report that until we have something to report.

BACK ON THE PLANET, THE GUNGAN SUB HAS FINALLY REACHED ITS DESTINATION, THE CAPITAL CITY OF NABOO.

THE DROID ARMY HAS CAPTURED THE CITY AND IS ESCORTING THE QUEEN AND HER CABINET TO A HOLDING CAMP.

THE JEDI USE THE FORCE TO MASK THEIR PRESENCE UNTIL...

...THEY JUMP FROM THE BALCONY AND ATTACK THE CAPTORS.

BLAST THEM!

ROGER, ROGER.

BEFORE THE DROIDS CAN REACT, THE JEDI SLICE THROUGH THEM.

AS THE SHIP ENTERS SPACE, IT COMES UNDER HEAVY FIRE FROM THE TRADE FEDERATION'S BATTLESHIPS THAT FORM THE BLOCKADE AROUND NABOO.

The shield generator's been hit!

THE SHIP'S ASTROMECH DROIDS ARE DISPATCHED TO TRY TO REPAIR THE DAMAGE. ONE BY ONE THEY ARE BLOWN AWAY UNTIL ONLY ONE, R2-D2, REMAINS...

...WHO QUICKLY LOCATES THE PROBLEM.

The power's back! That little droid did it! Deflector shields up at maximum!

WITH THE SHIELDS FULLY OPERATIONAL, THE QUEEN'S CRUISER LIMPS AWAY FROM THE BATTLESHIPS AND NEAR-CERTAIN DESTRUCTION, IN NEED OF SOME MAJOR REPAIRS.

HAVING LOST THE SHIP, THE VICEROY REPORTS TO DARTH SIDIOUS.

And Queen Amidala, has she signed the treaty?

She...has disappeared, My Lord. One Naboo Cruiser got past the blockade. My Lord, it's impossible to locate. It's out of our range.

Not for the Sith.

This is my apprentice, Darth Maul. He will find your lost ship.

ALTHOUGH R2-D2 MANAGED TO FIX THE SHIELD GENERATOR, THE HYPERDRIVE IS BADLY DAMAGED AND THERE IS NOT ENOUGH POWER TO GET TO CORUSCANT. QUI-GON AND OBI-WAN DECIDE TO LAND ON TATOOINE, A DESERT PLANET OUTSIDE OF THE FEDERATION'S CONTROL.

The hyperdrive generator's gone, Master. We'll need a new one.

That'll complicate things. Be wary, I sense a disturbance in the Force. Don't let them send any transmissions.

25

QUI-GON, ACCOMPANIED BY R2-D2 AND JAR JAR, SETS OUT TOWARD A SPACEPORT TO FIND THE NECESSARY PARTS TO REPAIR THE HYPERDRIVE.

WAIT!

Her Highness commands you to take her handmaiden with you.

No more commands from her highness today, Captain. This spaceport is not going to be pleasant.

The queen wishes it.

This is not a good idea.

AFTER A LONG WALK, THE GROUP ARRIVES AT MOS ESPA SPACEPORT AND HEADS TOWARD A SMALL BUILDING SURROUNDED BY JUNK.

We'll try one of the smaller dealers.

AS THEY ENTER, A BELL RINGS, ALERTING THE OWNER, A STUMPY, FLYING CREATURE NAMED WATTO.

<Ah, customers! Boy, get in here, now!>

AS THE CREATURE FLIES AROUND THE COUNTER TO TEND TO HIS CUSTOMERS, A BOY RUSHES IN.

<Watch the store! I've got some selling to do.>

Let me take you out back, sir. We'll find what you need!

WATTO LEADS QUI-GON OUT INTO THE MAIN YARD, LEAVING THE QUEEN'S HANDMAIDEN, JAR JAR AND R2-D2 WITH THE YOUNG BOY.

Are you an angel?

What?!

27

An angel! I heard deep space pilots talk about them. They're the most beautiful creatures in the universe. They live on the Moons of Iego, I think.

You're a funny little boy. How long have you been here?

Since I was three, I think. My mom and I were sold to Gardulla the Hutt, but she lost us betting on the Podraces.

You're a slave?!

No, I'm a person! And my name is Anakin!

OUTSIDE IN THE SPARE PARTS JUNKYARD...
A T-14 hyperdrive generator?
Thee in luck. I'm the only one hereabouts who has one. Saying of which, how's thee gonna pay for all of this?
I have twenty thousand Republic Dataries.
Republic credits are no good out here! I need something more real!
QUI-GON ATTEMPTS TO USE THE JEDI MIND TRICK ON WATTO.
I don't have anything else, but credits will do fine...
No, they won't. What, you think you're some kind of Jedi?
I'm a Toydarian! Mind tricks don't-a work on-a me...only money. No money, no parts, no deal!

AS THE TRIO WALKS THROUGH THE MARKET, JAR JAR SPIES A TASTY GORG DANGLING FROM A STRING.

Mmmmmmm! Mooie mooie!

WHEN JAR JAR'S TONGUE LASHES OUT AT THE GORG, IT CATAPULTS INTO A NEARBY CAFÉ...

...AND INTO THE LAP OF A VERY UNPLEASANT-LOOKING CHARACTER.

Huh?!

THE CREATURE LEAPS ACROSS HIS TABLE AND PINS JAR JAR TO THE GROUND.

<Is this yours?>

Who, mee-sa?

LUCKILY FOR JAR JAR, ANAKIN ARRIVES.

<Careful, Sebulba! He's a big-time outlander. I'd hate to see you diced before we race again.>

<Next time we race, boy, it will be the end of you. If you weren't a slave, I'd squash you now!>

<Yeah, it'd be a pity if you had to pay for me!>

GLARING AT ANAKIN, SEBULBA SLOWLY TURNS AWAY AND GOES BACK TO HIS SEAT AT THE CAFÉ.

OUT IN THE DESERT, A VICIOUS SANDSTORM IS BEGINNING TO SWELL.

This storm will slow them down.

It looks pretty bad.

CAPTAIN PANAKA RECEIVES A MESSAGE ON HIS RADIO.

Receiving a message from home.

We'll be right there.

The death toll is catastrophic! We must bow to their wishes. You must contact me!

It's a trick. Send no reply. Send no transmissions of any kind!

MEANWHILE, ON THE PLANET CORUSCANT, DARTH MAUL INFORMS LORD SIDIOUS THAT HE HAS FOUND THE QUEEN AND HER PARTY.

Tatooine is sparsely populated. If the trace is correct, I will find them quickly, Master.

Move against the Jedi first. You will then have no difficulty in taking the Queen to Naboo to sign the treaty.

At last we will reveal ourselves to the Jedi. At last we will have revenge.

You're a Jedi, aren't you? I saw your laser sword. Have you come to free us?

No, I'm afraid not. We're on our way to Coruscant, the central system in the Republic, on a very important mission.

How did you end up here in the Outer Rim?

Our ship was damaged and we're stranded here until we can repair it.

35

The prize money would more than pay for the parts they need!

Anakin, your mother is right. Is there anyone friendly to the Republic who can help us?

No, there is no other way. I may not like it, but... he can help you. He was meant to help you.

THE FOLLOWING DAY, QUI-GON RETURNS TO WATTO'S SHOP TO MAKE HIS PROPOSAL.

The boy tells me you want to sponsor him in the race. How can you do this? Not on the Republic credits, I think?

My ship will be the entry fee.

QUI-GON SHOWS
WATTO A HOLOGRAM
OF THE QUEEN'S SHIP.

A Nubian, huh? But
what will the boy ride?
He smashed up my Pod
in the last race!

Well, I have acquired a Pod in a game of chance.
The fastest ever built. If we win, you keep all
the money, minus the cost of the parts I need. If
we lose, you keep my ship. Either way, you win.

DEAL!

38

AS ANAKIN PREPARES HIS POD FOR THE RACE, QUI-GON CONTACTS OBI-WAN TO TELL HIM ABOUT THE PLAN.
What if this plan fails, Master? We could be stuck here a very long time.
Well, it's too dangerous to call for help, and a ship without a power supply isn't going to get us anywhere.
Also, there is something about this boy.
AS QUI-GON ENDS HIS TRANSMISSION TO OBI-WAN, SHMI JOINS HIM OUTSIDE.
You should be very proud of your son. He gives without thought of any reward.
Well, he knows nothing of greed. He has a...
He can see things before they happen. That's why he appears to have such quick reflexes. It's a Jedi trait.

He deserves better than a slave's life.

The Force is unusually strong with him. That much is clear. Who was his father?

There...there was no father. I carried him, I gave birth, I raised him... I can't explain what happened.

Can you help him?

I don't know. I didn't actually come here to free slaves.

SUDDENLY, THE CONVERSATION IS INTERRUPTED BY A DEAFENING ROAR AS ANAKIN POWERS UP THE PODRACER.

It's working! **It's working!**

ELSEWHERE, DEEP IN THE TATOOINE DESERT, A SMALL YET OMINOUS SHIP HAS LANDED.

THE CLOAKED FIGURE OF DARTH MAUL EMERGES...

...AND USING HIS ELECTROBINOCULARS, HE SCANS THE HORIZON.

THREE PROBE DROIDS HOVER DOWN THE SHIP'S RAMP AND SILENTLY SEARCH FOR ANY SIGN OF THE QUEEN AND HER PARTY.

THE FOLLOWING DAY, QUI-GON AND HIS GROUP MAKE THEIR WAY TO THE PODRACER HANGAR AT THE SPACEPORT ARENA.

I want to see your-a spaceship the moment the race is over. I warn you, no funny business!

You don't think Anakin can win?

Don't get me wrong, I have great faith in the boy. He's a credit to your race. But Sebulba there is going to win. I'm betting heavy on Sebulba!

I'll take that bet. I'll wager my new racing Pod against, say...the boy and his mother.

No Pod is worth two slaves! Not by a long shot!

We'll let fate decide. I just happen to have a chance cube here. Blue, it's the boy. Red, his mother!

AS WATTO THROWS THE CUBE TO THE GROUND, QUI-GON USES THE FORCE TO MAKE SURE THAT THE DIE ROLLS BLUE.

You won this small toss, outlander, but you won't win the race. So it makes little difference!

OUTSIDE, THE STADIUM IS PACKED.

Greetings! We have a big turnout here for the Boonta Classic, the most hazardous of all Podraces!

That's right! And our glorious host, Jabba the Hutt, has just entered the arena!

THE CROWD ROARS AS JABBA WAVES TO THEM FROM HIS PRIVATE BOX.

44

ON THE TRACK, SEBULBA QUIETLY LOOSENS A POWER COUPLING ON ANAKIN'S POD, THEN CASUALLY WALKS OVER TO ANAKIN...

<You won't walk away from this one, slave scum! You're bantha poodoo!>

Don't count on it, slime-ball!

QUI-GON HELPS ANAKIN INTO HIS POD.

You all set, Annie? Remember...concentrate on the moment. Feel, don't think! Use your instincts... May the Force be with you.

THERE'S A GROUND-SHAKING ROAR AS THE PODRACERS' ENGINES REV UP.

It looks like everyone's ready! Racers! Start your engines!

GO!!

45

THE BOONTA CLASSIC'S REPUTATION AS THE MOST TREACHEROUS COURSE IS WELL DESERVED. AS ONE BY ONE THE RACERS ARE ELIMINATED.

AAAAAAGH!!!

BY THE FINAL LAP, ONLY SEBULBA AND ANAKIN ARE STILL IN THE RACE.

ANAKIN NUDGES FORWARD, BUT SEBULBA IS HOT ON HIS TAIL.

SEBULBA'S EARLIER SABOTAGE PAYS OFF AS A WARNING LIGHT FLASHES ON ANAKIN'S DASHBOARD AND ONE OF HIS ENGINES SHUTS DOWN...

...AND SEBULBA RACES INTO THE LEAD.

Heh! Heh!

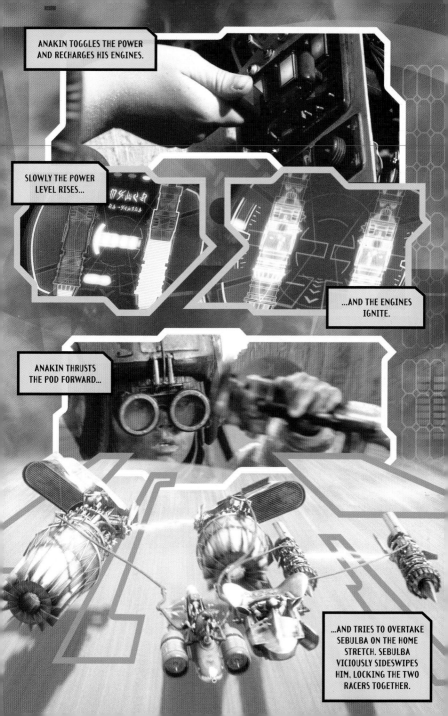

ANAKIN PULLS HIS POD AWAY AND SEBULBA LOSES CONTROL, PLOWING INTO THE GROUND. HIS ENGINES EXPLODE INTO A THOUSAND PIECES...

AAAAAGH!!!

...LEAVING ANAKIN FREE TO CROSS THE FINISH LINE, VICTORIOUS.

Hooray!

It's Skywalker! The crowd is going nuts!

BACK IN THE DESERT...

<Poodoo!>

Hooray, Annie!

50

I will come back and free you, Mom! I promise!

AND SO BEGINS ANAKIN'S LONG AND FATEFUL JOURNEY.

IN THE DESERT, A PROBE DROID REPORTS BACK TO DARTH MAUL.

MOMENTS LATER, THE SITH LORD CLIMBS ABOARD HIS SPEEDER BIKE AND SPEEDS TOWARDS THE SPACEPORT.

INSIDE THE SHIP...

Qui-Gon is in trouble! Take off and fly low!

THE SHIP FLIES OVER TO QUI-GON'S POSITION, PICKS HIM UP AND THEN BLASTS INTO SPACE, SAVING QUEEN AMIDALA FROM THE CLUTCHES OF THE SITH.

What was it?

I don't know...but it was trained in the Jedi arts. My guess is it was after the Queen.

WITH THE SHIP REPAIRED, THE JEDI CONTINUE ON THEIR MISSION TO DELIVER THE QUEEN TO CORUSCANT...

THE GLEAMING SHIP WEAVES ITS WAY THROUGH THE CONGESTED SKYWAYS OF THE CITY UNTIL IT REACHES A LANDING PLATFORM WHERE SUPREME CHANCELLOR VALORUM'S SHUTTLE HAS JUST DOCKED.

AS THE QUEEN DISEMBARKS, SHE IS GREETED BY THE CHANCELLOR AND SENATOR PALPATINE.

It is a great gift to see you alive, Your Majesty. May I present Supreme Chancellor Valorum?

Welcome, Your Highness. It's an honor to finally meet you in person. I must relay to you how distressed everyone is over the current situation. I've called a special session of the Senate to hear your position.

I am grateful for your concern, Chancellor.

AS PALPATINE LEADS THE QUEEN AND HER ENTOURAGE TO HIS QUARTERS, QUI-GON AND OBI-WAN MAKE THEIR WAY TO THE JEDI TEMPLE TO REPORT TO THE JEDI COUNCIL.

He was trained in the Jedi arts. My only conclusion can be that it was a Sith Lord.

AN UNEASY MURMUR RUNS THROUGH THE COUNCIL CHAMBER.

Impossible! The Sith have been extinct for a millennium!

I don't believe the Sith could have returned without us knowing.

Hard to see, the dark side is!

We will use all our resources to unravel this mystery. We will discover the identity of your attacker. May the Force be with you.

Master Qui-Gon... More to say have you?

I have encountered a vergence in the Force. A boy. His cells have the highest concentration of midi-chlorians I have seen in a life-form. I request that he be tested.

Bring him before us, then.

MEANWHILE, SENATOR PALPATINE AND THE QUEEN PUT THEIR CASE BEFORE THE GALACTIC SENATE.

Supreme Chancellor, delegates of the Senate...a tragedy has occurred on our peaceful planet of Naboo that has engulfed us in the oppression of the Trade Federation. I present Queen Amidala, the elected ruler of Naboo, who speaks on our behalf.

THE QUEEN TAKES THE PLATFORM AND ADDRESSES THE SENATE.

Honorable representatives of the Republic, the Naboo system has been invaded by a droid army belonging to the Trade Federation.

SENATOR LOTT DOD, THE TRADE FEDERATION'S REPRESENTATIVE, PROTESTS.

I object! There is no proof! We recommend a commission be sent to Naboo to ascertain the truth!

Queen Amidala, will you defer your motion to allow a commission to explore the validity of your accusations?

I will not defer! If this body is not capable of action, I suggest a new Chancellor is needed. I move for a vote of no confidence in Chancellor Valorum's leadership!

A ROAR OF APPROVAL FOR THE VOTE ECHOES AROUND THE CHAMBER.

BACK AT THE JEDI TEMPLE, QUI-GON AND OBI-WAN DISCUSS ANAKIN'S FUTURE.

The boy will not pass the Council's tests, Master. He's too old.

Anakin will become a Jedi. I promise you.

Don't defy the Council, Master. Not again.

I shall do what I must, Obi-Wan.

If you would just follow the code, you would be on the Council. They will not go along with you this time.

AS MASTER QUI-GON AND HIS APPRENTICE OBI-WAN REFLECT ON ALL THAT HAS HAPPENED, ANAKIN IS BEING TESTED BY THE JEDI COUNCIL.

What do you see?

A ship. A cup. A speeder.

ANAKIN CONCENTRATES ON THE HIDDEN IMAGES, THEN ANSWERS.

BACK AT PALPATINE'S RESIDENCE, THE QUEEN IS DEEP IN THOUGHT.

You-sa tinken you-sa people ganna die?

Gungans no dyin' without a fight. Wee-sa warriors. Wee-sa gotta grand army.

I don't know...

SUDDENLY, SENATOR PALPATINE AND CAPTAIN PANAKA WALK IN.

Your Highness! Senator Palpatine has been nominated for the position of Supreme Chancellor!

A surprise, to be sure. Your majesty, if I am elected, I promise to put an end to corruption.

Senator, this is your arena. I feel I must return to mine. I've decided to go back to Naboo.

Go back?! But, your majesty, be realistic! They will force you to sign the treaty!

I will sign no treaty, Senator! My fate will be no different from that of our people. Captain! Ready my ship!

THE JEDI RESPECTFULLY FOLLOW THE COUNCIL'S ORDERS TO ACCOMPANY THE QUEEN BACK TO NABOO.

THE SHIP LANDS IN THE FOREST TO AVOID DETECTION, AND JAR JAR IS SENT TO CHECK ON THE FATE OF THE GUNGANS WHILE THE OTHERS SET UP CAMP.

I'm sorry for my behavior, Master. It's not my place to disagree with you about the boy.

You have been a good apprentice and are much wiser than I am, Obi-Wan. I foresee that you will be a great Jedi Knight.

PADMÉ SUDDENLY STEPS FORWARD...

I am Queen Amidala. I'm sorry for the deception, but it was necessary to protect myself. Your Honor, our two great societies have always lived in peace. I ask you to help us.

?!

ANAKIN IS SHOCKED TO LEARN THAT HIS FRIEND PADMÉ IS REALLY THE QUEEN.

QUEEN AMIDALA DROPS TO HER KNEES IN A SHOW OF RESPECT...

No...I beg you to help us. Our fate is in your hands.

...AND SO DOES THE REST OF HER PARTY.

BOSS NASS LOOKS AT THE SCENE CAUTIOUSLY BEFORE ERUPTING INTO LAUGHTER.

HA! HA! You-sa no tinken you-sa greater den the Gungans? Meeee-sa lika this! Maybe wee-sa bein' friends!

THE TENSION IN THE AIR MELTS IN A SEA OF CHEERING AND SHOUTING AS THE NABOO AND THE GUNGANS FINALLY JOIN FORCES AGAINST A COMMON FOE.

LORD SIDIOUS, HAVING DISPATCHED DARTH MAUL TO NABOO, IS UPDATED ABOUT THE QUEEN'S PLANS.

This is an unexpected move for her...

It's too aggressive. Lord Maul, be mindful. Let them make the first move.

Yes, Master.

Almost everyone's in camps. A few hundred police and guards have formed an underground resistance. The Federation Army is also much larger than we thought.

Your Highness, this is a battle I do not think that we can win.

The battle is a diversion. The Gungans must draw the droid army away from the cities. Then we can enter the palace and capture the Viceroy. Without the Viceroy, they'll be lost and confused.

There is a possibility, with this diversion that many Gungans will be killed.

Wee-sa ready to do our-san part.

We will send what pilots we have to knock out the droid control ship orbiting the planet.
A well-conceived plan. However, there is great risk. The weapons on your fighters might not be able to penetrate the control ship's shields.
And there's an even bigger danger. If the Viceroy escapes, he'll return with another droid army!
That is why we must not fail to get the Viceroy. Everything depends on it!

THE GUNGAN SOLDIERS ACTIVATE GENERATORS TO CREATE A HUGE SHEILD OVER THE ASSEMBLED WARRIORS.

ON SEEING THE SHIELD IN OPERATION, THE DROID ARMY ATTEMPTS TO BLAST THE GUNGANS WITH THEIR HEAVY ARTILLERY.

OPEN FIRE!

ALTHOUGH POWERFUL, THE FEDERATION ARMY'S FIRE IS ABSORBED EASILY BY THE SHIELDS.

WITH THEIR ARMY OCCUPIED BY THE GUNGANS, ONLY A SMALL NUMBER OF TRADE FEDERATION BATTLE DROIDS ARE LEFT GUARDING THE PALACE, ALLOWING THE QUEEN AND HER PLATOON TO SNEAK IN.

There's the entrance!

SUDDENLY, THEY'RE SPOTTED.

THERE THEY ARE! BLAST THEM!

AS FIGHTING BREAKS OUT, THE QUEEN'S GUARDS BLAST THE BATTLE DROIDS' TANK AND KNOCKS THEM OUT.

AS THE QUEEN'S GUARDS MOP UP THE LAST FEW DROIDS IN THE MAIN PLAZA, THE REST HEAD INTO THE HANGAR, WHERE THEY ARE MET BY MORE DROIDS.

Get to your ships!

AS THE QUEEN'S GUARDS LAY DOWN SUPPRESSING FIRE, THE PILOTS RUSH TO THEIR FIGHTERS AND TAKE OFF TO DESTROY THE DROID CONTROL SHIP.

ANAKIN PUSHES SEVERAL BUTTONS IN THE COCKPIT. THE STARFIGHTER'S GUNS COME TO LIFE AND EASILY DESTROY THE DROIDEKAS...

...ALLOWING THE QUEEN TO ESCAPE.

Let's find the Viceroy!

UNFORTUNATELY, ANAKIN HAS ALSO ACTIVATED THE FIGHTER'S ENGINES.

It's on autopilot. Try to override it, Artoo!

AS R2-D2 FRANTICALLY TRIES TO OVERRIDE THE FIGHTER'S SYSTEMS, IT BLASTS OFF INTO SPACE.

BACK ON THE BATTLEFIELD, THE DROIDS' BATTLE TANKS STOP FIRING...

...AS THE BELLIES OF THE FEDERATION'S TROOP TRANSPORTS SLOWLY OPEN AND UNLOAD THEIR OMINOUS CARGO: THOUSANDS OF BATTLE DROIDS.

ON FOOT, THE DROID ARMY QUICKLY PENETRATES THE GUNGANS' SHIELD AND BEGINS A VICIOUS GROUND WAR.

BACK IN THE PALACE, THE DUEL CONTINUES. EVEN AGAINST TWO TRAINED JEDI, DARTH MAUL IS A FORMIDABLE OPPONENT.

QUI-GON PUSHES DARTH MAUL DOWN A CORRIDOR TOWARD THE PALACE'S GENERATOR CORE.

OBI-WAN RUSHES TO AID HIS MASTER...

...BUT AS HE REACHES THE END OF THE CORRIDOR, A TIMED SECURITY SHIELD ACTIVATES ITSELF, SEPARATING HIM FROM THE FIGHT.

QUI-GON DROPS HIS GUARD FOR ONE SECOND, AND THE SITH LORD STRIKES A DEADLY BLOW.

NOOOOO!!!!

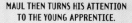

MAUL THEN TURNS HIS ATTENTION TO THE YOUNG APPRENTICE.

AS THE BEAM DISAPPEARS, A FURIOUS OBI-WAN LUNGES AT HIS ADVERSARY...

...BUT DARTH MAUL KICKS OBI-WAN AND FORCE-PUSHES HIM INTO THE GENERATOR CORE'S VENTILATION SHAFT.

THE JEDI APPRENTICE MANAGES TO GRAB ON TO A LIGHT IN THE SHAFT...

...AND DARTH MAUL KICKS HIS LIGHTSABER INTO THE SHAFT.

AS MAUL PEERS DOWN AT HIM, OBI-WAN NOTICES QUI-GON'S LIGHTSABER AT THE SITH LORD'S FEET.

USING THE FORCE TO GUIDE HIM, OBI-WAN SOMERSAULTS OUT OF THE PIT, SUMMONING QUI-GON'S LIGHTSABER, WHICH HE SWINGS WITHOUT HESITATION.

THE BLADE HITS ITS MARK.

?!!

MAUL'S BODY FALLS SILENTLY BACKWARD INTO THE PIT, HIS BODY SPLITTING NEATLY IN TWO, REVEALING THE FEROCITY OF OBI-WAN'S ATTACK.

WITH MAUL DISPATCHED, OBI-WAN RUSHES OVER TO QUI-GON.

Obi-Wan... promise me you'll train the boy...

THE JEDI MASTER'S BODY RELAXES, AND HIS EYES CLOSE FOR THE LAST TIME.

MEANWHILE, ANAKIN'S SHIP IS STREAKING INTO SPACE.

Look, Artoo! The autopilot is taking us to the droid control ship!

THE SURFACE OF THE CONTROL SHIP IS CRISSCROSSED WITH FURIOUS LASER FIRE AS THE NABOO PILOTS TRY TO BREAK DOWN ITS DEFENSES.

AS ANAKIN APPROACHES THE BATTLE, A DROID FIGHTER DROPS IN BEHIND HIM, GUNS BLAZING.

We're hit, Artoo!

ANAKIN'S SHIP NOSEDIVES INTO THE CONTROL SHIP'S HANGAR, WHERE IT SCREECHES TO A HALT...

...ATTRACTING THE ATTENTION OF A SQUAD OF BATTLE DROIDS.

Everything's overheated. This is not good!

ANAKIN TOGGLES A SWITCH TO RESTART THE FIGHTER'S ENGINES AND ACCIDENTALLY FIRES A PROTON TORPEDO.

THE FIGHTER'S ENGINES ROAR TO LIFE AS THE PROTON TORPEDO RUPTURES THE SHIP'S REACTOR CORE.

Let's get outta here!

THE STARFIGHTER ACCELERATES OUT OF THE HANGAR.

THE FIGHTING OUTSIDE IS INTERRUPTED AS A CHAIN OF EXPLOSIONS RIPS THROUGH THE BODY OF THE CONTROL SHIP.

It's blowing up from the inside! All pilots move out of range!

JUST AS THE NABOO PILOTS REACH A SAFE DISTANCE, THE CONTROL SHIP IS TORN APART BY AN ENORMOUS EXPLOSION.

WITH THE VICEROY CAPTURED AND HIS ARMY VANQUISHED, THE NABOO RECLAIM THE CITY.
I think you can kiss your trade franchise goodbye!
Now, Viceroy, you'll have to go back to the Senate and explain all this.
AS THE VICEROY LEAVES, SENATOR PALPATINE'S SHUTTLE ARRIVES FROM CORUSCANT.
We are indebted to you for your bravery, Obi-Wan Kenobi. And you, young Skywalker...
...we will watch your career with great interest.
Congratulations on your election, Chancellor.
Your boldness has saved our people, Your Majesty. It is you who should be congratulated. Together we shall bring peace and prosperity to the Republic!

LATER THAT DAY, YODA ARRIVES ON NABOO TO SPEAK WITH OBI-WAN...

Confer on you the level of Jedi Knight, the Council does...

...but agree with your taking this boy as your Padawan learner, I do not.

Master Yoda, I gave Qui-Gon my word. I will train Anakin. Without the approval of the Council, if I must.

Qui-Gon's defiance, I sense in you. Need that, you do not.

Agree with you, the Council does. Your apprentice, Skywalker will be.

AS NIGHT FALLS, EVERYBODY GATHERS IN THE FUNERAL TEMPLE TO PAY THEIR RESPECTS TO QUI-GON JINN.

What will happen to me now?

The Council has granted me permission to train you. You will become a Jedi, I promise.

ELSEWHERE, MACE WINDU AND YODA REFLECT ON THE DAY'S EVENTS.

There is no doubt that the mysterious warrior was a Sith.

Always two there are. No more, no less. A master and an apprentice.

But which one was destroyed, the master or the apprentice?

90

WITH THE PLANET LIBERATED FROM ITS OPPRESSORS, THE GUNGANS AND THE NABOO JOIN TOGETHER TO CELEBRATE THEIR NEWFOUND PEACE.

CLIMBING THE STEPS, BOSS NASS RECEIVES THE GLOBE OF PEACE FROM THE QUEEN TO MARK A NEW UNDERSTANDING BETWEEN THEIR PEOPLES.

HE HOLDS THE GLOBE ABOVE HIS HEAD AND THE CROWD LETS OUT A DEAFENING CHEER.

YAHOO!!

To be continued...

PODRACERS OF THE BOONTA CLASSIC

MANUFACTURER:
RADON-ULZER/ANAKIN SKYWALKER
PILOT: ANAKIN SKYWALKER
COCKPIT LENGTH: 3.15 METERS
ENGINE LENGTH: 7 METERS

RADON-ULZER 620C

MANUFACTURER: ORD PEDROVIA
PILOT: GASGANO
COCKPIT LENGTH: 2.72 METERS
ENGINE LENGTH: 9.71 METERS

CUSTOM SPECIAL

MANUFACTURER: MANTA RAMAIR
PILOT: ALDAR BEEDO
COCKPIT LENGTH: 5.28 METERS
ENGINE LENGTH: 10.59 METERS

MANTA RAMAIR MARK IV

COLLOR PONDRAT

MANUFACTURER:
COLLOR PONDRAT
PILOT: SEBULBA
COCKPIT LENGTH:
3.96 METERS
ENGINE LENGTH:
7.47 METERS

EXELBROK XL 5115

MANUFACTURER: EXELBROK
PILOT: ODY MANDRELL
COCKPIT LENGTH: 3.76 METERS
ENGINE LENGTH: 8.69 METERS

JAK RACING J930 DASH-8

MANUFACTURER: JAK RACING
PILOT: EBE ENDOCOTT
COCKPIT LENGTH: 3.05 METERS
ENGINE LENGTH: 9.55 METERS

MANUFACTURER: VULPTEREEN
PILOT: DUD BOLT
COCKPIT LENGTH: 3.66 METERS
ENGINE LENGTH: 7.92 METERS

VULPTEREEN 327

TURBODYNE 99-U

MANUFACTURER: ELSINORE-CORDOVA
PILOT: WAN SANDAGE
COCKPIT LENGTH: 2.06 METERS
ENGINE LENGTH: 5.03 METERS